DR XARGLES
BOOK OF
EARTH MOBILES

Text copyright ©1991 by Jeanne Willis. Illustrations copyright ©1991 by Tony Ross.
This paperback edition first published in 2004 by Andersen Press Ltd. The rights of Jeanne Willis and Tony Ross to be identified as the author and illustrator of this work have been asserted by them in accordance with the Copyright, Designs and Patents Act, 1988. First published in Great Britain in 1991 by Andersen Press Ltd., 20 Vauxhall Bridge Road, London SW1V 2SA. Published in Australia by Random House Australia Pty., 20 Alfred Street, Milsons Point, Sydney, NSW 2061. Colour separated in Switzerland by Photolitho AG, Zurich.Printed and bound in Italy by Grafiche AZ, Verona. All rights reserved.

10 9 8 7 6 5 4 3 2 1

British Library Cataloguing in Publication Data available.

ISBN 1 84270 369 2

This book has been printed on acid-free paper

DR XARGLE'S BOOK OF EARTH MOBILES

Translated into Human by Jeanne Willis
Pictures by Tony Ross

Andersen Press · London

Good morning, class. Today we are going to learn
how earthlings travel.

Earthlings can reach a top speed of one mile in three minutes in their vest and pants.

The oldest form of transport known to them is the Dobbin.

To catch a Dobbin, put a square of sugar on your hand and creep towards him. Grab his hairdo and fling your legs in the air.

When startled Dobbins do a handstand.

This earthlet is able to travel at many miles per hour down a steep slope. He has attached wheels to his footwear, but no brakes.

Here he is again in the casualty department.

The bicycle is popular. The earthling must hang on to the prongs and move his knees up and down.

He must put a metal clip around his leg to prevent
the bicycle eating the trouser.

Earthhounds can run as fast as a bicycle with pigmeat in. If one approaches, press the ting-a-ling and prepare to eject.

A car has many eyes. It winks at its friends with these. It has a tail. Out of this comes stinkfume.

Every Sunday, the earthling strokes the car with a piece of soft material. He lies underneath it and tickles its tummy. For Christmas, he buys it two woolly cubes with dots on.

If someone bumps the car, the earthlings must go out and wave his fist in the air. He then calls the other earthling the son of a baboon and insists that he buys some spectacles.

A boat is made from a tree and a sheet tied to a stick with string.

When the ocean is bouncy, the earthlet goes green.

Here are some phrases I would like you to learn.
"Yo ho ho and a glass vessel with rum in it!"
"Hello sailor!"
"Earthling overboard!"

An aeroplane has a tail, some wings and a beak but no feathers.

The earthlings are only allowed to get on if they smile. Then, they are tied to the chairs so they can't escape.

If the earthlings stop smiling, they are made to eat leather in glue, boiled plants and a cake with squashed flies in it. A tinful of boiling water and leaves is then poured over their knees.

A train is a long metal tube stuffed with earthlings.

When the train starts, the earthlings on the seats cover themselves with newspaper. The others swing from the ceiling.

Sometimes a family of moohorns have a picnic on the metal rails. The earthlings lean out of the window and shout at the moohorns and the driver.

Then along comes the Tickets Please. He gets out his snipper and ruins the tickets.

That is the end of today's lesson.
Get into the spaceship quickly and put on your
disguises. We're going to visit planet Earth and have
a ride on a train.

Matron has managed to book us tickets for the
Ghostie Express.